To Ben, my pants-tastic illustrator ~ CF

For Ruth, with all my love ~ BC

**SIMON AND SCHUSTER**

First published in Great Britain in 2010 by Simon and Schuster UK Ltd
1st Floor, 222 Gray's Inn Road, London WC1X 8HB
A CBS COMPANY

A CIP catalogue record for this book is available from
the British Library upon request

ISBN: 978-1-84738-569-7 (HB)
ISBN: 978-1-84738-570-3 (PB)

Printed in China

1 3 5 7 9 10 8 6 4 2

# Aliens Love
# Panta Claus

Claire Freedman & Ben Cort

**SIMON AND SCHUSTER**

London  New York  Sydney

The aliens are excited,
As tomorrow's Christmas Day,
So instead of stealing underpants,
They're giving them away!

They jump into their spaceships — whee!
And whizz off to Lapland,
Full of the Christmas spirit,
To give Santa Claus a hand.

The aliens read the letters out,
From all the girls and boys,
And, just for fun, they add a pair,
Of pants in with their toys!

In Santa's busy workshop,
They cause lots of jolly snickers,
When dressing up the little elves,
In fancy, frilly knickers.

The reindeer wear their underpants,
Lit up all bright and glowing,
With neon pants to light the way,
It helps show where they're going!

Great! Santa's nearly ready,
But, shhh, when he turns his back,
The aliens swap a spotted pair,
Of bloomers for his sack!

"Ho-ho-ho!" laughs Santa,
But his smile turns to a frown,
He won't be going anywhere,
His sleigh has broken down!

It's aliens to the rescue,
With their spaceship for a sleigh,
So reindeer bells a-jingling,
Here comes Panta Claus — hooray!

They hover over rooftops,
And it really is fantastic,
How Santa shoots down chimneys,
On a rope of pants elastic!

The aliens follow Santa,
As he tiptoes to each bed,
They take down all the stockings,
And tie knickers up instead.

They decorate our Christmas trees,
With festive knicker cheer,
And leave out underpants that say,
"An alien woz 'ere!"

Then, mission done, they fly back home,
To plan their next attack,
So hold on to your underpants,
The aliens **will** be back!